This Story is a Lie

PRAISE FOR BENJAMIN DEAN

'A scandalous thriller.' THE *GUARDIAN*

'My favourite kind of YA. Benjamin Dean is a welcome addition to the UK YA scene and has written a royal triumph.'
JUNO DAWSON, AUTHOR OF *HER MAJESTY'S ROYAL COVEN*

'Scandalous, funny and deliciously compelling!'
CATHERINE DOYLE, CO-AUTHOR OF *TWIN CROWNS*

'All hail this exquisitely twisty, delightfully queer mystery.'
CHELSEA PITCHER, AUTHOR OF *THIS LIE WILL KILL YOU*

'A compelling thriller that stays with you
long after you've finished reading.'
KATHRYN FOXFIELD, AUTHOR OF *GOOD GIRLS DIE FIRST*

'More jaw-dropping, OMG-twists than even the
most salacious tabloid journalist could create.'
ERIK J. BROWN, AUTHOR OF *ALL THAT'S LEFT IN THE WORLD*

'One page-burning scandal after another.
Benjamin Dean is YA royalty.'
FEMI FADUGBA, AUTHOR OF *THE UPPER WORLD*

'A scandalous, twisty mystery that had me on
the edge of my seat gasping for more.'
KATE WESTON, AUTHOR OF *MURDER ON A SCHOOL NIGHT*

'A twisty thriller that kept me guessing until the very end.'
LEX CROUCHER, AUTHOR OF *GWEN AND ART ARE NOT IN LOVE*

'Addictive, compelling, and utterly delicious.'
SIMON JAMES GREEN, AUTHOR OF *NOAH CAN'T EVEN*

'The scandal of the season!'
ABIOLA BELLO, AUTHOR OF *LOVE IN WINTER WONDERLAND*

This Story is a Lie

BENJAMIN DEAN

SIMON & SCHUSTER

First published in Great Britain in 2025 by Simon & Schuster UK Ltd

1 3 5 7 9 10 8 6 4 2

Simon & Schuster UK Ltd
1st Floor, 222 Gray's Inn Road
London WC1X 8HB

www.simonandschuster.co.uk
www.simonandschuster.com.au
www.simonandschuster.co.in

Simon & Schuster Australia, Sydney
Simon & Schuster India, New Delhi

A CIP catalogue record for this book
is available from the British Library.

PB ISBN 978-1-3985-4267-9
eBook ISBN 978-1-3985-4266-2
eAudio ISBN 978-1-3985-4268-6

Typeset in Bembo by M Rules
Printed and Bound in the UK using
100% Renewable Electricity at CPI Group (UK) Ltd

MIX
Paper | Supporting
responsible forestry
FSC® C171272

For those who need an escape from the world around them – this is yours.

WORLD BOOK DAY ®

World Book Day's mission is to offer every child and young person the opportunity to read and love books by giving you the chance to have a book of your own.

To find out more, and for fun activities including video stories, audiobooks and book recommendations, visit worldbookday.com

World Book Day® is a charity sponsored by National Book Tokens.

NOW

I know you want to ask me what happened that day. Everybody wants to know. I see the stares in the hallway, hear the whispers behind my back. Even the teachers are looking at me with something that's not quite pity – more curiosity, like they want the answers too. But the truth is, I feel like I hardly know anything. It's a blur in my mind at best and a completely black void at worst. Maybe it's for the best that I can't remember everything.

I don't want to live this nightmare any more.

Still, I see you all watching. Even now, when you know the outcome, you won't let me move on. Not until I tell you my side of the story. So, if that's what it takes, have it your way. Let me take you back to the start. But just one important thing before we get started.

Remember, their story was a lie.

TWO
WEEKS AGO

The swell of Year Eleven students swept me down the corridor in the direction of the auditorium, penning me in from all sides. There was nowhere to go but forward and I started to feel claustrophobic in the midst of the chaos. It was already so hot in there, the summer air stale and stuffy, but the couple of hundred bodies pushing in the same direction added to the heat. I loosened my tie and undid my top button, hoping to find some elusive breeze, but there was nothing.

'Hey, Harley. Madness, isn't it?' Peter McGregor

materialized by my side, his pale face violently flushed, but his green eyes bright and full of excited spark. He was using his planner as a fan, although the only success it seemed to be having was in making his dark brown curls resemble more of a bird's nest than it already did. I grimaced in response, still trying to desperately find some oxygen. I wouldn't say we were friends, exactly – more outsiders who banded together out of pure necessity from time to time (AKA when we desperately didn't want to be the only one without a lab partner).

'Excited?' Peter asked. Before I could answer, he enthusiastically ploughed on. 'I heard one of last summer's winners has just been cast in a movie. And remember the one from Scotland a few years ago who was, like, a promising tennis player or something? Apparently, he got a scholarship to a college in America. He could be the next big sports star, according to the programme's website.'

'Oh, I'm sure they're not biased or anything,' I murmured.

'Not the point,' Peter carried on. 'Those people

who won are out in the world *doing* things. Living their dreams. Getting a spot on the programme is, like, guaranteeing the future you've always wished for.'

I laughed and gave Peter a nudge. 'Wow, you really have been reading their website. Wanna get their slogan tattooed on your forehead or something?'

Peter rolled his eyes. 'You won't be saying that when you get your spot and become the youngest artist in history to make a million quid or whatever.'

'See, I don't need dreams – you've got them for me.' I grinned, but my smile quickly faded. 'Nah, man. It all sounds nice in theory, but ...' I shrugged. 'The programme has two places available. There's almost two hundred people in our year. You do the maths. I'd rather save myself the disappointment.'

Peter's eyes widened. 'You mean you *didn't* put yourself forward? Have you lost your mind?'

I laughed at the incredulous look on Peter's face. 'Oh, come on, you can't tell me you genuinely believe either of us actually has a chance. The artist and the writer? We're the *last* people they're giving the opportunity to.'

'Hey! Less of the *we*. I personally think we have as much chance as anybody.'

Before I could respond, I noticed the claustrophobic pressure around me lightening. For just a second, I felt like I could breathe again. When I turned around, I soon realized why.

The Perfect Four, as I'd imaginatively nicknamed them, were walking down the corridor. Or *gliding*. Floating. Whatever people who aren't mere mortals do. The sea of students quite literally parted for them, somehow making room as if they were royalty. I guess at Hardbridge Academy, they kind of were.

Theo, Annabella, Billie and Oliver.

They looked at complete ease, laughing and joking with each other, barely registering that people were almost fighting to move out of their way. I swear, if you looked close enough, you'd have probably seen a golden shimmer emanating from them as they passed.

'And *that's* why I didn't put my name forward,'

I whispered to Peter as they disappeared through the double doors into the auditorium. Everybody rushed to follow suit. 'The programme filters the candidates down to the best four, who then make it through to the interview stage. You think *any* of us are competing with them?'

Peter looked like he wanted to argue, but he deflated quickly with a defeated sigh. 'Fair point.' He scowled, then added optimistically, 'But you never know.'

'If it makes you feel better, you'd be my pick,' I said. 'You know, if the other four were all off sick or something.'

Peter laughed and we shuffled into the auditorium, finding seats on the tiered benches near the back. The Perfect Four were, of course, holding court in the middle. It was amazing how people seemed to gravitate towards them, like they were four suns and the rest of us merely dying plants that desperately needed their light. Each one of them looked completely relaxed, as if waiting to find out if your dreams might come true was a daily occurrence for them.

Or like they knew they'd already won.

I guess they were just so used to having their way. Talent and brains could open some doors, sure, and they had those in abundance. Theo with his football. Annabella with her acting. Billie with her singing. Oliver with his intelligence. But wealth and power, which all of their parents had more than enough of, paid to make those opportunities a certainty. The big difference between most of us and them: if they didn't make it onto the Rising Stars programme, they would still be all right. *More* than all right. Nobody else in the room could say the same thing.

Rising Stars was a global corporation with influence in a ton of lucrative industries. Their production company had funded Oscar-winning movies; their record label boasted some of the biggest pop stars in the world; the sports teams they sponsored had won every major league, title and competition on offer. And that was just the tip of the iceberg. From actors to writers, directors to artists, singers to politicians, sports stars to business moguls, there wasn't an industry that Rising Stars hadn't conquered.

Their summer programme was their way of *giving back*. Or their way of not looking like a greedy corporation that seemingly owned half the world and all its power. Every year, the UK branch chose one school and selected a shortlist of four students, which was eventually whittled down to two winners who Rising Stars would invest in to make their dreams come true. And, even though I could still hardly believe it, Hardbridge Academy had beaten every school in the country to be the lucky one. Suddenly, dreams that felt so far away and out of reach now seemed *possible*.

If you were one of the Perfect Four anyway.

Every student in Year Eleven was crammed into the hall to find out who the final candidates would be, and even though the deal was all but sealed in my eyes, there was an excited chatter buzzing among us. Even the teachers had shown an interest, hovering around the edges of the room, making whispered bets with each other that they didn't think we could hear. I heard Mr Bennett put a tenner on Theo Atwick to be one of the winners. Miss Dern said that was like betting Usain

Bolt would win in a hundred-metre sprint against toddlers. I would've been offended, but she had a point.

The judges sat in armchairs onstage, three representatives from the Rising Stars programme holding our fledgling dreams in their hands, ready to grant them or crush them at a moment's notice. They had clipboards, all official-looking. Even though I hadn't entered my name, my heart still fluttered with adrenaline and suspense, which only multiplied when a middle-aged woman with neat black hair stood up and tapped the microphone. The silence was immediate and so thick, I could feel it pressing down all around us.

'Welcome, Hardbridge Academy, to the Rising Stars candidate selection!' she said grandly, beaming out at us all. There was some polite applause. Peter was watching her raptly. 'My name is Maria Turner and I work with Rising Stars. As many of you know, the Rising Stars summer programme is a prestigious celebration of the young talent we have in this country. We've been finding and nurturing that talent for over thirty years now, taking students such as yourselves from dreamers to ... actors, singers, sports stars, artists, designers, entrepreneurs, politicians ... even one prime minister! And now, Hardbridge Academy, it's your turn.'

The room watched Maria in awe, as if she herself could wave a magic wand and make every dream in there come true. Even I was starting to get invested, forgetting everything I'd just said to Peter ten minutes before.

'The applications this year have been excellent – honestly, some of the best I've seen in years – which has made our job *super* hard.' Maria gestured to the other judges behind her, who nodded in agreement. 'But after much consideration, we've managed to narrow it down to our top four! So, without further ado ...'

The tension in the air was suffocating. Everybody in Year Eleven sat up a little straighter, leaning towards the stage, desperate to know if their dreams would suddenly be in reach. Maria relished the dramatics a little longer, before finally reading out the first name.

'Theo Atwick!'

'Of course the golden boy's first,' Peter muttered beside me.

Tall and lean, with dark, close-cropped curls and brown skin a few shades lighter than my own, captain of the football team (although he was excellent at rugby and cricket too), warm and funny, and every teacher's favourite (even if he was never top of the class), Theo just had that charisma – the kind that could persuade you to buy oxygen. If you had to place a bet on who was going to become the next David Beckham someday, your money would be on him. Mine too, actually. And Mr Bennett's.

There was no hint of nerves as Theo climbed the stairs and sauntered into the spotlight to face the crowd, waving like he was King of Hardbridge Academy. He commanded the stage as if it was his home, as if the spotlight wasn't dazzling him because it was made for him. He nodded his head once with half a smile that reeked of confidence and sat in the first chair like it was a throne.

'Annabella Penn!'

'And there goes the ice queen herself,' Peter said. I guessed he was giving his commentary to distract from his own nerves about how much he wanted this.

Ice queen was a fitting description for Annabella. Everything about her was cold and sharp, from her pointed nose and chin to her pale blonde hair that looked almost silver. Even her complexion reminded me of the cold, unforgiving snow of January. Her expression often mirrored the same. While Theo wanted to be loved and adored, Annabella wanted to be revered and feared. Of course she was talented; there was no doubt about that. In the Year Eleven summer stage show a couple of weeks earlier, she'd all but saved the day. Heather Baxter, who'd been playing the other leading role, had spectacularly thrown up moments after she'd stepped onstage. The show might've been ruined, but Annabella shone so bright, people almost forgot about it, reducing every parent in the audience to tears with her monologue. Come to think of it, I think *I* cried too.

But there was no denying that people were

straight up scared of Annabella. She was blunt and cold, and she clearly didn't give a damn if you liked her or not. Annabella *knew* she was better than you, and she wasn't going to waste her time pretending otherwise.

'No point in announcing the other candidates,' Peter muttered beside me, clearly miffed. 'They'll be the two winners, as always. But let me guess, next is voice of an angel—'

Confirming his theory, Maria announced: 'Billie Bradley!'

The third member of the Perfect Four, Billie Bradley was the musician of the group, with dark brown skin, warm eyes to match and black braids entwined with strands of hair dyed white and silver. She could sing, she could play the piano and guitar, she could write her own songs. With so much talent, it'd be easy to hate her, but she was friendly enough. I suppose it's easy to be nice to others when nobody poses a threat to what you do. She glided to the stage, hiding a small smile as she went.

That left one spot. I glanced over at Oliver, the

last of the Perfect Four, now basically alone. His girlfriend, Violet, was the only one beside him, although even she was more focused on the stage and the people on it. The other students around him who had begged for his attention before were now ignoring him. I wondered if they ever really looked at him or just *past* him in search of the other three.

It was fair to say that Oliver was the least impressive, somewhat of an outsider in the group. Sure, he had the status and wealth and some popularity. But he had lived in Theo's shadow, especially, his whole life. They were like brothers. Oliver was the moon to Theo's sun. He shone bright in his own subtle way, but he never dazzled like Theo did. He was the quiet one, always on the periphery, with pale skin, fox-coloured floppy hair and round glasses that framed a watery-blue gaze. He was top of his classes with a real encyclopaedic brain that could probably take him to Downing Street one day. But getting a perfect score in maths wasn't as dazzling a talent as what the others could offer. And it definitely couldn't compete with Theo's all-round brilliance.

At that moment, his shoulders were tense, his jaw locked like he was trying hard not to grind his teeth. His hands were curled into tight fists, the knuckles white and threatening to pierce the skin. As I watched him, I realized he *didn't* know if he had this in the bag. He was as nervous as everybody else who had put their names forward. All that confidence he exuded when he stood with Theo, it was merely bravado. A cover-up.

'And the final candidate is . . .'

There was a pause, and Peter leaned in to whisper: 'You were right, the Perfect Four win again. I can't believe I thought it'd be different.'

'Harley Matthews!'

Cue pandemonium. The auditorium went wild. The rule book was out of the window and so too was human decency. We were animals now, fighting and snarling and scrapping. It was a fight to the death and may the best monster win.

Or that's what I imagine might've happened anyway. Of course, it didn't. But damn, I was sure full-blown chaos was about to break out. I swear every head in that room turned and found me. I froze in my seat, positive I hadn't heard her correctly. She couldn't have said my name. She must've got it wrong, or maybe she was playing some kind of prank and any second now she would start laughing along with the rest of the school.

But nobody was laughing.

'Oh my god, Harley, it's you!' Peter breathed next to me. 'I thought you didn't enter?'

I frowned, my heart starting to gallop in my chest. 'I *didn't*.'

The edges of my vision were blurring. It felt like I was no longer attached to my own body, but instead floating just outside of it. Onstage, the Perfect Four – or was it three now? – were frowning, their ever-present haloes skewed slightly. Finally, the swelling pressure punctured and an excited, adrenaline-soaked fervour broke free around the auditorium. Peter pushed me to stand up, nudging me towards the stage where my fate awaited.

My legs trembled, barely able to support me as I walked. On the stage, the spotlights were burning hot, triggering an anxious sweat, which broke out on my neck and down my back. Maria was waiting with a big grin, her arms spread wide as if she was about to hug me. Instead, she offered her hand, and I shook it. My palms were so sweaty, they slid out of her grasp. I took my seat, slightly off to the side, suddenly so aware of my body and how *everyone* was looking at me. The centre of attention was a landmark I usually avoided at all costs. I was the introverted artist, happiest with a paintbrush in hand and only myself for company. This was my worst nightmare.

I chanced a glance at the other three, but they were doing a great job at ignoring my presence, staring offstage instead. I followed their eyeline and realized they were looking at Oliver, still sitting in the audience with Violet. But his eyes weren't meeting theirs.

They were glaring right at me.

I shook hands with enough people to last a lifetime, teachers and judges congratulating me with pats on the back. 'I'm not surprised in the slightest,' Mr Briggs, my art teacher, announced when he made it to the stage. 'You have a very special talent.'

Mr Briggs had always been my biggest supporter, my work adorning the walls of his classroom. There was the landscape I'd painted in Year Eight when I was experimenting with water colours, the still-life paintings from Year Nine and, my most recent and proudest project of all, a series of sketches revealing two faceless boys, always just out of reach of the other, depicting how it felt to have a crush on someone but never being brave enough to tell them. I guess you could say it was inspired by my real life.

Hanging on the walls of Hardbridge Academy today – tomorrow, the walls of the Tate Modern, Mr Briggs used to joke. I was glad he believed in me so much, because I often didn't believe in myself.

The rest of the Year Elevens began to file out of the auditorium, heading for lunch, while the chosen candidates were herded into a small room just off the stage and instructed to each take a seat around a large table. Once we were all seated, the judges began speaking about the next steps. It basically involved an interview and a presentation on our talent. I was in too much of a whirlwind to ask any questions – I just nodded and went along with it. But then Maria dropped a bombshell.

'One last thing before we let you go.' Her smile was short-lived, replaced by the shadow of a grimace. My blood pulsed in my ears. What now? 'Unfortunately, I have some bad news. Funding for the summer programme has been ... difficult, to say the least, over the last few years, but this year in particular has been tough. As a result, I'm afraid there are no longer two winning spots available. There will now only be one.'

It was like every breath of oxygen had been sucked out of the room. We all glanced at each other, taking in our competition. Theo. Annabella. Billie. Me. Three of us would have our dreams dashed. Even Theo, who usually radiated such confidence, looked a little uneasy. I sat back in my chair in disbelief. But, as I looked across the table and took in my new rivals, I realized one important thing. The newly coined Perfect Three could only be friends if they weren't in competition. Now they posed a direct threat to each other.

All bets were off.

When the meeting was done, I left the room, finally free and alone. I didn't fancy being stared at by every student over lunch, so I swerved up a short flight of stairs next to the auditorium and ducked into the bathroom, splashing water on my face. It was quiet here, everybody else no doubt piled into the cafeteria on the other side of school. For a moment, I felt like I could try and catch my breath.

Maybe the adrenaline had eliminated my hunger, but lunch with everybody watching didn't seem all that appealing. Instead, I decided to avoid it altogether and sat on the lid of the toilet in the last cubicle reading the latest social media post from a boy in the year above, who I had a bit of a crush on. Before I knew it, I was browsing pictures of his holiday to Tenerife in 2019 to celebrate his aunt's fiftieth birthday, until it was time to leave for fourth lesson.

At the row of sinks, I studied myself in the mirror, hoping to find someone else looking back – someone who wore my skin with more confidence, like they deserved to be on the shortlist. But all I saw was myself, blood drained from my deep golden complexion and anxiety hiding just beneath the surface of my dark brown eyes. Would everybody else see it too? I took a deep breath, checked myself in the mirror one last time, and left the bathroom.

I didn't see it at first.

I was coming down the stairs, mind a blur of everything that had just happened, in my own little world. But then my foot stepped off the last stair, and I was standing right in the middle of it.

I tutted to myself when I realized I had white chalk on my shoe. I wiped it off, brushing my hands to get rid of the residue. But then I looked down properly and saw there was more. It had been etched into the floor at the bottom of the stairs in the shape of—

I gasped, jumping away from it. When I looked back and saw it properly, everything around me stopped.

The outline of a person was positioned at the bottom of the stairs like some kind of crime scene. It was white, but there was a scribble of red chalk around its head. *Blood.* And next to that were some words. I couldn't read them from my vantage point so, even though everything was telling me to run, I crept closer until the words came into focus.

HARLEY MATTHEWS.

My own name, taunting me. It was written in small, neat capital letters above the outline's head. But that wasn't all. Below my name was a message, and it chilled me to the bone.

NEXT TIME, IT'LL BE YOU.

Fear doused itself over me, enveloping me entirely. My knees buckled and my head began to swim. I thought I was going to pass out, the edges of my vision blackening. I stumbled backwards, breathing heavy, heart thundering. I whipped around, suddenly scared that someone might come up behind me. But there was nothing. It was just me and my outline, together and completely alone.

I came to my senses quickly. I couldn't stay here. Not if the person behind it was nearby. Maybe they were watching me now. Or maybe it was a prank – just someone messing about, equally surprised that I'd made the shortlist. I tried to convince myself that was true, but, in my heart, I knew this was serious. I had to show someone.

I ran down the corridor, looking in every classroom I passed for a teacher. But there wasn't one in sight; they were all at lunch on the other side of school. Before I knew it, I'd done a mini loop of the music and drama department, ending up back where I'd started.

But now, my body was gone.

As if it had simply never existed, the outline and its accompanying words had vanished. There was nothing there. I shook my head, because that was impossible, and crouched down, grazing my hand over the floor. When I checked, there was a thin layer of white chalk coating my palm. But other than that, there was no evidence that anything had ever been there at all.

Fourth lesson was maths. My heart rate still hadn't returned to normal after seeing that chalk outline of myself. I tried to push it from my mind, to focus on anything else, but it was all I could think about. As I approached the classroom, I debated pulling myself out of the Rising Stars race. I hadn't even put myself forward! If someone else wanted it that bad, they could have it as far as I was concerned.

I was so lost in my own world that I nearly crashed into someone at the door. Just my luck, it was Oliver, who I was certain hated my guts for taking the spot he wanted so bad. Did he hate me enough to want to push me down some stairs too?

He was accompanied by his girlfriend Violet, and Theo, who were busy talking about the latest episode of *Just a Little Fun*, a TV murder mystery about an after-school club being stalked by a killer. It was all any Hardbridge Academy student with even a crumb of popularity had been talking about for weeks. I still hadn't seen it.

Oliver's glare darkened, piercing straight through me. I tried to stutter something, anything, to make things less awkward, but I couldn't find any words. What if it was *him* who'd left the chalk outline to freak me out?

'See you later, Ollie,' Theo called over his shoulder as he and Violet broke away, heading down the corridor to their own classroom. Their heads were bent close together, still chattering about the show. Oliver looked after them, then turned his glare back to me. He tutted, shook his head, and barged through the open door.

'If he tries to kill you, I'll have your back.' Peter appeared beside me, staring after Oliver. 'I can't promise I'll be any help, but company's better than nothing.'

I huffed a laugh, although I didn't find it very funny. The chalk outline of my own body was still at the front of my mind. As we found seats near the back corner, dropping our bags under the desk, I decided to tell Peter everything. This didn't feel like something I should keep to myself.

'What. The. Hell,' Peter hissed when I'd finished.

'Creepy, right?'

'That's one way of putting it. Sick and twisted is

another. You have to tell someone! Like, a teacher or something.'

I grimaced. 'I don't know. It feels like making it a bigger deal than it is. I'm sure it's just someone trying to freak me out.'

'Textbooks out!' Mr Bennett called. 'Turn to page thirty-six.'

Peter began to flip through the pages of his book while I leaned back in my chair. As Mr Bennett started droning on about geometry, Peter moved in a little closer and nodded in the direction of Oliver, who was doodling in the back of his exercise book.

'If anybody had a motive to mess with you a little . . .'

I watched Oliver myself for a moment. I couldn't really argue with Peter's theory, but would Oliver take it that far?

'You really didn't put your name forward for the programme then?' Peter asked.

I shook my head. 'Nope.'

'Well, not to freak you out, but –' Peter grimaced – 'if you didn't put your name forward, then who did?'

I'd been asking myself the same thing, but there were no obvious answers I could think of. All I knew was that it was already causing more trouble than it was worth.

Of course, things were about to get worse. That was when the first blog post went live.

Mr Bennett was putting us all to sleep with his monotonous voice. I had my head resting in the palm of my hand, fighting to keep my eyes open. Unsuccessfully. My head felt fluffy on the inside, hazy and struggling to pull focus. I only vaguely heard the ping of a phone notification. It came from the other side of the room, near the window. Rookie error to have your phone on loud, especially in Mr Bennett's class. He pursed his lips and swivelled in the direction of the sound.

'Who has the phone? They should be switched off. Whoever it belongs to, hand it over.'

There was silence, nobody willing to fess up. In the quiet, there was a vibration, this time closer to me, from the table to my right. Mr Bennett didn't hear it and, with his attention focused elsewhere,

Maisie King risked a peek at her phone screen. I watched her eyes widen, glee dancing in them as her eyebrows shot up her forehead. She nudged Katie next to her and showed her whatever had her excited. I couldn't explain why, but I started to feel hot, the knowledge that something was being shared for everyone to see. But what?

'What's going on?' Peter murmured beside me, clearly catching wind of the buzz pulsing in pockets of the room. He checked Mr Bennett wasn't watching and pulled out his own phone, glancing at the email notification on his screen. I watched him click a link, then read for a second before his mouth dropped open. 'No way.'

'What is it?'

Peter was too engrossed in whatever he was reading to answer. Unable to bear the wait, I reached for my own phone, hoping I hadn't been left out of the loop. Sure enough, there was an email notification waiting for me. *You've got mail,* it announced. I clicked the link, which opened up a mini blog post. With a flutter of curiosity mounting in my chest, I began to read.

<u>CREAM</u> OF THE CROP

What's up, Hardbridge Academy! Your
resident know-it-all here. Tough luck to
everyone missing out on the Rising Stars
shortlist. I know it sucks, but hey, I've
got something that might just cheer you
all up. Shall we play a game? Let's call
it Guess Who. Here's how it works:

I give you a clue.

You guess the person it's related to.

The truth is revealed.

And boy, do I have some secrets to share.

So, let's get started. Here's your first clue ...

This person has two faces and loves
pretending to be somebody else. In fact,
they love it so much, they'll make sure

nobody else can compete with them.
This person doesn't cry over *spilled*
milk. But someone else sure does.

Guess who . . .

More secrets soon.

There was no name attached to the message, just a simple smiley face, as if the author hadn't just turned the world of Hardbridge Academy upside down. Sure, gossip always roamed the halls of our school, traded like currency. But this was different. Someone was claiming to know secrets about other people while hiding behind a shroud of anonymity. Despite the thrill of gossip, it felt . . . *terrifying*. Like we were all being watched from the shadows.

'Who sent this?' I whispered to Peter, even though I could clearly see for myself that the post was completely anonymous and the email address was just random numbers and letters.

'Beats me,' Peter murmured. '*Resident know-it-all*? I mean, that could be anybody.'

True. Narrowing that down with no clues would be nearly impossible in a school of a thousand students. But we *did* have clues to guess the answer to the puzzle.

'Then who are they talking about?' I tried, changing tack as Mr Bennett successfully confiscated the phone on the other side of the classroom and restarted his lecture. 'Is it someone we know?'

Peter frowned, watching the other students in the classroom whispering among themselves. When someone pointed towards the front row, he shot up straight, fizzing with excitement.

'Oh my god.' He grabbed his phone and re-read the blog post, then jabbed a finger at the screen. 'Two faces. Loves pretending to be someone else. Almost like they're playing a character . . .'

My head whipped around, finding Annabella. I couldn't quite see her face, but she was fidgeting in her chair at the front of the class, fiddling with loose strands of her hair. If I didn't know any better,

I'd have guessed she'd read the post for herself and was . . . nervous?

'But what's with the dairy joke?' I murmured. 'I don't get it.'

Peter rolled his eyes and slapped my arm as if I was being purposefully stupid. 'Come on! Who do you know who's intolerant to dairy? Someone who may or may not have gone to A&E because they were violently throwing up on the day of the summer stage show . . .'

It came to me like a lightning bolt. 'Heather Baxter?' Peter nodded, his eyes flicking back and forth between me and Annabella, who now had her hand in the air.

'Yes, Annabella?' Mr Bennett asked.

'I need the bathroom.'

Mr Bennett sighed. 'You're excused.'

The entire classroom watched Annabella get up and all but run for the door. The moment it closed, there was an eruption of whispers. Mr Bennett scolded a few students near the front row, but Peter just lowered his voice and continued.

'The only person who could've got anywhere

close to being as good as Annabella onstage was Heather. Coincidence much that she suddenly vomits the moment she steps onstage? Everybody knows she's seriously intolerant to dairy. What if someone – say, Annabella – slipped something into her drink to make sure she wouldn't be able to shine too brightly? With her out of the way, Annabella was basically the saviour of the whole show.'

The clues were there for us all to see. But could it be true? Would Annabella really go that far to make sure nobody could compete with her? I glanced at my phone again, the smiley face at the end of the blog post taunting us all, and my brain snagged once again on my very first question.

Who the hell was behind this?

Both Annabella and Heather were called into the headteacher's office during fifth lesson. Rumour had it Annabella was denying everything, adamant that it wasn't true and just some silly little post. But that didn't stop the whole school from gossiping about it, taking it for bible. It didn't exactly help her case that Heather confirmed her sudden illness before the stage show *might've* been triggered by her dairy intolerance, which she'd been confused about at the time.

People were also speculating about the identity of the blogger. Some names had been thrown around, theories created out of nothing but dislike for someone else. Nothing like this had happened at Hardbridge Academy before. It certainly didn't look like the situation would die down anytime soon.

By the end of the day, I was drained and exhausted. I was halfway to an exit, re-reading the blog post over and over again because, like everyone else, I was invested in the whole thing, when someone called my name. I turned to find Mr Briggs, my art teacher, pacing towards me.

'Harley, how are you doing?' he asked as he approached. A smile twitched beneath his salt-and-pepper moustache.

'Good thanks, sir. How are you?'

Mr Briggs waved his hand as if it was a silly

question. 'Same old, same old. Not much changes for an ageing man like myself. Retirement is all I've got to look forward to now.' He chuckled to himself. 'Anyway, I'm glad I caught you. I wanted to congratulate you once again on getting shortlisted for the Rising Stars programme. It's a really big deal and, well ...' He seemed a little nervous, which immediately put me on edge. 'Well, I just wanted to say I'm sorry if I stepped out of line, but it was me who put you forward for it in the first place.'

The words tumbled out of him like he'd been struggling to hold them in. He looked a little embarrassed, blushing around the ears.

'I really must apologize – it was rude of me to do it on your behalf. It's just, I recalled a conversation we'd had on the topic, and I knew you were putting yourself and your talents down again. You weren't going to apply for fear you'd be rejected and I just ... well, I couldn't let that happen. I really wanted you to succeed. Your talent can't be put to waste, Harley.'

I was speechless and taken aback, but more than

anything, I was grateful. Mr Briggs looked nervous as he waited for me to say something, so I quickly cleared my throat.

'Thank you so much, Mr Briggs. I'm very glad you did. I owe you, big time.'

Mr Briggs looked relieved, his shoulders relaxing. He laughed to himself, as if he'd believed I'd be angry about the whole thing. Then he frowned.

'Do you not have somewhere to be? I saw Billie five minutes ago – she said there was a get-together you all had to attend.'

It came back to me in a flash. There was a Rising Stars meeting scheduled for today, after school, and I was already late.

'Thanks again, Mr Briggs!' I called over my shoulder as I legged it down the corridor. I arrived at the classroom breathless and flustered to find Billie was the only other person there.

'Hey,' she said warmly, immediately putting me at ease. 'Congrats on getting that final spot. I've heard your work is really great.'

I tried not to blush as I took my seat. 'Thanks. I

mean, *everybody* has heard your talent. Your voice is incredible.'

Billie had the grace to look modest, at least. 'Thank you. That's really kind.' A small, almost shy smile tugged at her lips. 'Here's hoping that voice gets me where I wanna be in life.'

There was silence for a moment, one I desperately wanted to fill. This was the first time we'd ever spoken. I wanted to know more.

'Where do you want it to take you?' I asked.

Billie glanced out of the window, lost in her daydreams for a moment. 'Just, away from here. I want to see the world and everything it has to offer. That'd be nice. Better than here anyway.'

'You can say that again,' I said, and we both laughed. 'I'm sure you've seen plenty of the world already though, right?'

Her eyes narrowed slightly, although more out of curiosity than annoyance. 'What makes you say that?'

I squirmed in my seat slightly. 'Well, you know . . . you and your friends are all pretty well off, right? I'm sure you go on, like, holidays and stuff . . .' I trailed off, embarrassed. Billie breathed a gentle laugh, but there wasn't really any humour in it.

'I think everybody assumes that because I'm friends with those guys, I must be rich too.' She looked me in the eye and shook her head. 'Far from it. I've just known them since we were kids. My dad works for Theo's family.'

I felt like the world's biggest idiot for assuming. But Billie didn't make me feel bad about it. Her smile widened as she went back to gazing out the window. 'Honestly, don't worry about it,' she said. 'One day, maybe I'll be rich like them too.'

'Hey, what's up,' Theo said, bowling through the door and taking a seat next to Billie. He gave me a nod, which seemed pretty neutral, so I gathered he at least didn't dislike me for ruining the Perfect Four's party.

'So, what's your deal?' he asked, looking in my direction when he was settled. His tone was curious, no hint of malice. 'You're an actor? That's your thing?'

I felt my eyebrows crease. Actor? I'd hardly call

pulling a sick day every now and then worthy of an Oscar. Theo watched my face and frowned himself.

'You were in the winter play, right? You played ...' He paused abruptly and I could see the realization dawning on him at the same time it crashed into me. He'd got the wrong person. He didn't even know who I was. Billie blushed for him, but Theo wasn't embarrassed. He just shrugged it off with a laugh.

'I'm an artist,' I said quietly. 'I draw and paint. That's my thing.'

Theo nodded and said, 'Of course,' like he'd known all along.

'Where's Bel?' Billie murmured to Theo after a moment or two. 'Did you see her this afternoon?'

Theo glanced at me as if I was intruding on a private conversation. I looked the other way and pretended I wasn't listening.

'Not since fifth when she was pulled out of class,' he said in a low voice. 'Haven't seen her since. I'm sure she'll be here in a minute.'

But before that minute could pass, Maria walked

through the door, beaming at us all and taking her seat at the head of the table. 'How are we all doing?' she asked, settling into her chair.

'We're all great, thank you,' Theo said, as if someone had appointed him as our group leader. He'd turned on that showmanship charisma, although up close, it kinda just looked like kissing butt. Still, Maria didn't seem to mind. In fact, she was charmed.

After some small talk and another congratulations on making it this far, Maria clasped her hands and said, 'Well, let's start. As you kn—'

'Sorry,' Billie interjected, before Maria could get any further. 'Shouldn't we wait for Annabella? She's not usually late, but I'm sure she won't be much longer.'

Maria gave Billie a sympathetic smile. 'Ah, yes – Annabella. Well, there's no use in me keeping secrets from you. I'm sure you'll all hear about it soon enough.' She paused, looking at each of us in turn. 'The judges have been alerted to an online post concerning Annabella. I'm sure you've all read it, but those accusations were *very* serious. We've spoken to your headteacher, as well as Annabella herself, and we've decided it's best to drop her from the shortlist, at least while the matter is being resolved. We'll hold her space until we have the full picture.'

Billie and Theo looked shocked, their jaws dropping in unison. I might've laughed in any other situation, but I knew mine had done the same. *What?!* It felt like a joke, some kind of prank being played on us, but Maria looked deadly serious.

'The Rising Stars programme is very prestigious. Our winning candidates are a representation of us when they step out into the world, and as a result, we cannot accept any . . . unsavoury behaviour. We must protect the institution and our core values, or what we stand for will be tarnished. I hope you can all understand that.'

Her words were only met with silence. She nodded as if the matter was closed and reassessed her notes, but she seemed to think of something else and looked up again.

'I'm sure there will be no further issues, but let

this be a gentle warning – the programme will not stand for any behaviour that could reflect badly on us. *None*. I would hate to take away this opportunity from any of you, but we won't hesitate to act accordingly, should we be forced to.' She tried to break the tension with a smile. 'But I'm sure we'll have nothing to worry about with you three. Any questions?'

We all solemnly shook our heads and Maria continued, talking about the interviews we'd have in a few days' time. But I struggled to focus on what she was saying. One person was now out of the race and all I could think about was the blog post which was responsible. Whether what it said was true or not, it had possibly ruined this opportunity for Annabella, and it'd promised that there were more secrets to come. That left one glaring question.

Who would be its next target?

The next day, the school still abuzz with gossip about Annabella, I bumped into Peter. He fell into step beside me, yapping about the wild theories he'd heard about since the blog post had gone live. Since everybody had assumed the post was about Annabella, speculation continued on *who* was behind the blog itself. Peter was fond of the theory that a teacher had written it, although he admitted ten seconds later that the idea was dumb.

'Annabella might've got bumped from the Rising Stars shortlist,' I said, when he paused to take breath. Peter gasped, spluttering to find an appropriate reaction. I laughed at the look on his face as I put in the combination for my locker and started unloading the heavier textbooks from my rucksack.

'I guess the programme doesn't want to be associated with someone who could potentially start poisoning people when they feel threatened,' Peter mused.

'You don't say,' I replied sarcastically.

Peter leaned back against the bank of lockers, staring out the window opposite. 'It's all a bit crazy, isn't it?'

'The post?'

Peter nodded and we started to walk up the corridor towards our form room. 'But not just that. It said there'd be more secrets. Do you think it's about . . .' He trailed off, looking awkwardly at the floor.

'About what?'

He swallowed, trying to find the right words. When he looked at me, I thought there might be sympathy hiding behind his eyes. 'Well . . . do you think it's going to be about the whole school? Or, you know . . .'

It clicked, what he wanted to say but couldn't without making me panic. Too late for that, I guess. 'Or will it just be about the Rising Stars candidates,' I finished for him. Suddenly, it felt a little too hot, like a fire was chasing after me through Hardbridge Academy.

Peter forced out a laugh, waving a hand in front of his face like we were talking nonsense, but I could tell he didn't believe that, which only made me panic more.

'Maybe the person behind the post is the same person who put your name forward for the programme,' Peter said, thinking out loud.

'I doubt Mr Briggs has much to gain by becoming

XOXO, Gossip Girl,' I said with a laugh. 'He found me yesterday and told me it was him who put my name forward. He said he didn't want me to waste my talent, or something equally as mortifying.'

Peter laughed. 'Well, you'll have him to thank when you're rich. Maybe he'll demand ten per cent for being the one to ...' Again, Peter trailed off. The corridors had started to empty out, leaving only a few stragglers behind. I followed his eyeline to the end of the hallway, where four people were stood huddled close together at the bottom of the art department stairs. I'm not a body language expert, but things weren't exactly looking friendly.

Theo, Annabella, Billie and Oliver were deep in conversation, serious looks etched into their faces. Theo was saying something to Annabella, but I couldn't quite hear him. She looked like she'd stopped crying a few minutes before, but right now, there was nothing but pure fury in her eyes.

'You expect me to believe that one of you isn't behind this!' Her raised voice flew down the corridor towards us as we hovered by our form room, rooted to the spot. Annabella scoffed, then turned her anger

46

on Theo. 'Pretty convenient, don't you think?'

'I don't know what you're talking about, Bel,' Theo said. 'You're being ridiculous.'

'Ridiculous?!' Annabella screeched. 'What's *ridiculous* is that you expect me to think this is all some coincidence. What, thought I might beat you to a place in the programme and couldn't face the fact that you might not be as good as you think you are?'

I'd never seen the dark expression that clouded Theo's face on him before. He was usually so calm and collected, confident and unruffled. But right now, he was simmering.

'That's absurd, Bel,' Oliver added.

Annabella whirled on him, jabbing her finger into his chest. 'Oh, of *course* you'd stand up for him. You've been living in his shadow for so long, you should start paying rent. I bet he probably paid you to do his dirty work for him. Better yet, you probably did it for free like a good little puppy.'

Oliver's face shifted, his own quiet rage matching Annabella's, but she didn't stop there.

'You've always been jealous of me! Jealous of

all of us. You can't stand the fact that you have *no* talent beyond being able to recite what a maths textbook says. Here's the truth – you were *never* going to make it onto the programme. *Ever.* So this doesn't concern you.'

There was a silence that draped itself over the corridor, the four of them glaring at each other, friendships fully fractured.

'Oh my god,' Peter whispered beside me, but in the quiet of the hallway, the Imperfect Four heard and whirled around to face us. I had to give it to them, even in the midst of an argument, they stood together to face outside enemies.

'Let's get out of here,' I murmured to Peter, and all but fell into the safety of our classroom.

'The Perfect Four, falling apart at the seams,' Peter whispered as Mrs Preston, our form tutor, gave us a warning look for being late. 'Who would've thought it?'

I mulled over what we'd just heard. 'You really think one of them wrote the blog?'

Peter thought about it. 'I'm not sure, but what I *do* know is that people will do anything to get what they want, even if it means stepping on friends to get there. The world's a selfish place, man.'

I snorted. 'Yeah, thanks for the reminder.'

The first blog post was still being discussed all over school, which is why everybody was surprised when another one dropped so soon. The link was sent around before lunchtime, in the middle of my history lesson. This time, there was no notification ping, but I soon began to notice the bowed heads of students clearly reading from their phones and a murmured excitement. Immediately, my heart started racing as I dug out my own. *You've got mail.* I clicked the notification and began to read.

THE COLOUR *PURPLE*

What's up, Hardbridge Academy. Me again. Bet you didn't think you'd be hearing from me so soon, but I know how much you loved my last post, so I didn't want to leave you hanging too long.

Fancy a new game? Of course
you do. How about this…

Every heir needs their spare, and
this friendship is no different. These
two best friends have so much in
common, they're practically siblings.
They even love the same _colour_!

Guess who…

The classroom was abuzz, so much so that Mrs Double had to shout to be heard above the noise. She carried on talking about the Tudors, but the whispers didn't stop, and I knew immediately why.

The first post had required a little more thought to untangle, but it seemed that this time, the Hardbridge Academy gossip had made things a little easier. In fact, it was so simple, the answer was in the title of the post itself.

The Colour Purple.

I doubted we were talking about the book here. But the clue was the colour itself. And what colour was related to purple? *Violet*. As in, Violet Gamble, the girlfriend of Oliver. *The heir and his spare* had to be talking about Oliver and Theo. Was the post suggesting Theo was more than friends with Violet?

I thought back to seeing Theo and Violet yesterday, outside our maths classroom. They'd been talking about *Just a Little Fun* so intently that they didn't even notice me and Peter. In fact, they barely seemed to notice Oliver. Could they really be so blatant? Or was the post lying, trying to sow distrust between friends?

No offence to Mrs Double, but I didn't have a single thought about the Tudors for the rest of the lesson. All I could think about was the post and, just as importantly, who the hell was behind it all. One post was a scandal. But two? That was ruin. Someone was out to take people down and it wasn't lost on me that the first two targets were on the Rising Stars shortlist. That left two questions.

Would there be more?

And would I be next?

I didn't have secrets to hide – it wasn't like I'd poisoned someone or taken another person's boyfriend. But that didn't stop the questions, confusion and dread taking root in my gut, burrowing deep. I hadn't even wanted to be a part of this circus in the first place. Now, I was in the middle of it all.

When the lunch bell rang, the class finally erupted into shouts and gasps and, weirdly, glee. Everyone was thrilled to have another morsel of gossip to cling on to, and it was swelling at an impressive rate, snowballing to encapsulate *more* scandal. People were saying they'd seen Theo and Violet alone together in town. Some said it was a milkshake date; others said the cinema. By the time I reached the lunch hall, the consensus was: Theo Atwick had stolen his inferior's girlfriend.

'Did you see the post?!' Peter threw himself into the seat next to me in the cafeteria, brimming with excitement. 'Violet and *Theo*?! There's no way that can be true.'

I shrugged. 'Why not? Didn't you see them yesterday, outside Mr Bennett's class?'

'I was more focused on trying to protect you from Oliver.'

I chuckled. 'Yeah, fair point.'

Peter craned his neck to peer over the tables in the cafeteria, his eyes finally landing on the seats in the middle that were usually unofficially reserved for the Perfect Four. Their table was empty.

'None of them have shown up for lunch,' Peter mused, shaking his head in disbelief. 'If you'd have told me last week that their friendship group would be falling apart at the seams, I wouldn't have believed you.'

I had to agree. They'd been so close for so long, sitting on their little perches above us mere mortals, gliding through life with the ease and confidence of people who didn't have a worry in the world.

Oh, how things had changed.

'Some of them have shown up,' I corrected, nodding in the direction of the opposite corner. Annabella was sitting with a small group of girls I was sure she'd never spoken to a day in her life before now. A smirk twisted her lips as she spoke, the girls surrounding her gazing up adoringly as if she was their queen. She looked smug, and I assumed it had something to do with the fact she was now out of the gossip crossfire. Well, that, or the fact she'd clearly gotten away with her dairy stunt because there was no way to prove she'd actually done it. Losing her place on the Rising Stars shortlist would sting, but Annabella knew better than anybody that, either way, she'd be okay in the end. Her family's wealth and power would make sure of that.

'Is that Billie over there?' Peter asked, looking past Annabella's table to one a few places along. Sure enough, Billie was sitting with a group of friends she played music with from time to time. She smiled as the others spoke, but she kept shooting worried glances around the hall. 'Dare I say, the Perfect Four are no more?'

Before I could say anything, the noise surrounding us quickly died down to a deathly silence. I looked over my shoulder to the cafeteria doors where Theo had just walked in, his usual bravado and showmanship dented. He looked sullen, his jaw clenched and eyes hooded. It was strange to see him walk in alone – usually he was surrounded by his friends, or at the very least a bunch of admirers. But here he was, walking in by himself, his golden glow entirely extinguished. How the mighty had fallen.

'What are you looking at?' he suddenly snapped to Lewis Draper, a boy in our year. Lewis was nowhere near Theo's level socially and, before, might've wilted on the spot. But now he smirked, full of bravado.

'What's your favourite colour, Theo? I heard it's *violet*.'

A few of his buddies snickered. Theo looked furious, set to pounce. I had no doubt he was ready for a fight, but before he could take a step, Mrs Hansen, our headteacher, intervened with a stern expression on her face. The cafeteria fell silent once more as she glared at us all.

'It has recently come to my attention that there are certain messages being spread around the school,' she said, her voice booming across the hall. 'We will *not* have this kind of behaviour at Hardbridge Academy. Rest assured, we will be looking for the culprit and they will be in *serious* trouble.'

With one final scowl, Mrs Hansen marched out of the cafeteria. Theo watched her go, but his eyes soon caught on something else. There, standing in the cafeteria doorway, was Maria and the other two judges from the Rising Stars programme, grimly watching on. Theo tried to raise a smile, but it didn't reach his eyes.

'I've decided I think you're going to win.'

Peter leaned into the locker next to me with a crash and no hello, making me jump. He laughed, watching the students go by. It was the next morning and first lesson geography beckoned.

'Thanks for the vote of confidence, I guess?'

Peter turned to look at me properly. 'Well, think about it. Annabella has been dropped for poisoning people—'

'Allegedly,' I interjected. 'And I don't think slipping dairy into someone's drink, even if they're lactose intolerant, counts as actual poison.' Peter kept talking as if I hadn't said anything.

'. . . and Theo is a homewrecker who has apparently stolen his best mate's girlfriend.'

'Again, allegedly. We don't actually know if any of that's true.'

Again, Peter ignored me. 'Which leaves you and Billie. If you ask me, that's a pretty fair fight. But I'd give you the edge. Maybe.' He thought about it for a few more seconds before changing his mind. 'Actually, I'm not sure. Billie nearly brought me to tears when she sang Olivia Rodrigo's "drivers license" in the talent show last year.'

He had a fair point, there was no arguing about that. He wasn't entirely right though.

'Not so fast – Theo *might* be a homewrecker, but he's still in the race as far as I know.'

'What?!' Peter looked aghast. 'So you can't give someone a little sip of milk, but you *can* steal their girlfriend and that's completely fine? *That* won't tarnish the reputation of the programme?'

'I mean, it doesn't look great, that's for sure. But I guess maybe the judges think that situation is more . . . immature kid stuff? It's not on the same level as sending someone to A&E.'

Peter thought it over. 'Okay, fine. I don't like it, but I suppose you have a point. I still think you're gonna win though. Good people always win in the end.'

I snorted. 'Let's not forget someone drew the literal outline of my body at the bottom of some stairs with the message *next time, it'll be you*. I wouldn't say that's winning. I'd say that's me at the very top of Oliver's kill list.'

Peter's laugh dropped immediately, his eyes widening as he looked over my shoulder. A pulse of panic reverberated through my body as I slowly turned my head. Behind me, at his locker, was Oliver himself. It was fair to say, he didn't look happy.

'Careful spreading lies like that, Harley,' he muttered darkly, slamming his rucksack into his locker. 'It might be you whose world is turned upside down next.'

Peter squeaked beside me. So much for back-up. I muttered a hurried apology and spun on my heel, heading in the completely wrong direction for geography. I just wanted to escape Oliver's death stare. When I chanced a glance over my shoulder before I turned the corner, he was still glaring after us.

'Yep, definitely at the top of his kill list,' Peter said, slightly breathless. 'And did you hear that stuff about your world turning *upside down*? Almost like he's planning on pushing you down some stairs.'

It was supposed to be a joke to lighten the mood, but we both looked at each other, neither one of us laughing. If anything, it just made me feel worse because ... well, what if Peter was right?

We made our way to geography, claiming seats at the back. Mr Jenkins had one of those slow, deep voices that could put you to sleep in sixty seconds flat, and since my spot was in the far corner, I made use of my blazer as a pillow to *rest my eyes* for ten minutes.

When Mr Jenkins set us a task from the Year Eleven textbooks, I realized I'd forgotten mine, so I ducked into the store cupboard at the back of the room, just behind my chair. I found the relevant textbook on a high shelf, then shut the door behind me, noticing Peter looking at me with an innocent but perplexed expression. Typical Peter, always lost in his thoughts. I took my seat again, wondering if this geography lesson would actually be the cause of my death instead of being pushed down a flight of stairs.

A couple of minutes passed and one of the student volunteers from Year Nine appeared at the classroom door, timidly knocking. Mr Jenkins called for her to enter and she shuffled inside.

'Harley Matthews, there's a phone call waiting for you at reception. And Peter McGregor, you have a dentist appointment.'

I perked up, frowning at the call of my name. Everybody in the class looked around to find us, which didn't exactly make me feel better. Fighting a blush, I grabbed my rucksack and stood up with Peter, exiting our classroom and following the volunteer to the front desk. The receptionist smiled and gestured to the phone.

'There was a message from your dad,' she said in my direction. 'Some kind of emergency. Asked you to call him back as soon as possible. And Peter, your mum called to say she'll be outside in five, so feel free to take a seat.'

'Why can't your dad just get you on your mobile?' Peter asked as I reached for the phone on the desk.

I scoffed. 'Try telling him that. He still thinks emails are the cutting edge of technology. I think he's the only human alive who prefers using the house phone. My mum thinks he's bonkers.'

Peter chuckled. 'See you at lunch then? Apparently, I'm not allowed to take the rest of the day off for a dentist appointment. Barbaric, if you ask me.'

'Agreed. I'd recommend the rest of the week off, personally.'

'Thank you!' Peter rolled his eyes with a grin.

He took a seat behind me while I dialled the number for my house. It rang half a dozen times before someone answered. I turned my back on Peter and said hello in a quiet voice.

'Did you want me, Dad?' I listened for a minute, then shook my head in disbelief. 'Maybe next time don't pull me out of a lesson if it isn't an emergency! I'll see you at home.'

I hung up, groaning under my breath.

'Everything okay?' Peter called.

'Apparently, it can wait until I get home tonight.' I rolled my eyes. 'See you at lunch then.'

'Yeah, see ya.'

I started back towards Mr Jenkins's classroom, scrolling on my phone through art inspiration for my next piece that I'd use in the interview stage for Rising Stars. I still hadn't really figured out what I was going to say, but I had always been better with pencils and paintbrushes than with words, so I was hoping my work could do some of the talking for me. I wanted to show them something that felt personal, something that revealed the loneliness I sometimes felt being a Black gay kid in school, and the hope I had for a life with freedom and companionship in the future. It was going to be tough to express, but I was up for the challenge.

I was so preoccupied that I almost missed the first one. And the second one. In fact, I would've carried on walking if I hadn't kicked them into a flutter as I was going. I tutted to myself, checking to see what had gotten in my way, and that's when I saw the posters. They were everywhere, scattered all over the corridor floor. I was about to bend down and pick one up when I realized some had been pasted to the front of the lockers. I could see a couple of words had been emboldened and underlined, written in red text to grab the eye. As I got closer, I knew something was wrong.

GAME OVER

Over the last few days, someone has been spreading stories and they've been getting away with it. Well, not any more. If people are going down, I'm **dragging her down too**.

The person behind the anonymous blog posts is **Billie Bradley**.

And she's hiding **secrets** of her own.

To everybody reading this, watch your purses and wallets.

Teachers included. Billie's got a bad
habit of taking **<u>what's not hers</u>**.

First the blog entries. Now posters from *another*
culprit accusing Billie of being behind the secrets
spilling forth online. The breath caught in my
throat. A second anonymous person hiding
themselves while delivering scandal. Were they
scared their secret was coming next and so got in
there first?

And *Billie*? That couldn't be true. Could it? Billie
was bright and bubbly, by far the friendliest of the
Perfect Four. She'd been so nice when I'd spoken
to her at the Rising Stars meeting. Sure, I could
imagine the other three doing anything to get on
top, but Billie was different, wasn't she?

Except, she was one of *them*. She always had
been. Billie had never felt threatened before, but
Rising Stars had changed that. They were supposed
to pick two people – now only one – for the
programme, and it had turned her closest friends
into her biggest rivals. Theo was a definite for
one of the spots in everybody's eyes, and people

just assumed Annabella would take the second. Had Billie thought the same and decided to do something about it? The fractures in the Perfect Four's friendship had been forming since the candidates for Rising Stars were announced, but did Billie want the place on the programme so bad that she'd betray her friends like *that*?

And to top it off, the accusation that she was a thief too? I could hardly believe it.

Did that mean that the anonymous posts and games were over, if Billie *was* the culprit behind them? And if she was stealing things, would that be grounds for suspension from school? I guessed there might not be any proof, but figured surely she was at least out of the race for the Rising Stars programme. If Annabella had been dropped with no proof of poisoning Heather, this had to be the same punishment, if not worse.

If that was the case, then ... did that only leave me and Theo in the running?

Before I could think about it too much, the bell rang, and students started to stream out of classrooms. I watched one person pick up a poster from the floor, and then another person and another, until there were frenzied shouts up and down the corridor. Before I'd even made it to my second class, it seemed like the whole school had heard the gossip – Billie Bradley was a thief, and she was betraying her best friends.

I debriefed with Peter over lunch the moment he was back from the dentist. He was equally shocked at the thought that Billie, of all people, could be behind it, while also miffed that he'd missed all the chaos because of a filling. I pulled one of the posters from my bag and gave it to him as a keepsake. He must've read it a hundred times before lunch ended.

The afternoon passed with little to no fanfare, but at the end of the day, as students streamed through the doors still discussing the drama from earlier, including me and Peter, I was tapped on the shoulder. I turned to find Maria, smiling.

'Do you mind if we have a quick chat? I promise it won't take very long.'

'I can wait if you want?' Peter said.

I shook my head. 'All good. I'll see you tomorrow.'

I followed Maria up a flight of stairs, Peter watching us go. When we reached the classroom, she gestured to the desk and took a seat herself. I took the one opposite, clasping my hands in my lap.

What now?

'I'm glad I caught you before you left. I just wanted to discuss the programme with you after some . . . recent developments.'

I assume she meant the absolute mayhem that had been unfolding over the last few days. It'd certainly been a ride, and one, I'm sure, Maria and the other judges were desperate to get off. No doubt they were regretting ever choosing our school. They certainly wouldn't be coming back; I'd put money on that.

'As you're probably aware, there have been some . . . rumours, let's say, regarding the other candidates in the running for the spot on this year's programme. It's put Rising Stars in a rather difficult position, not least because, as I said to you before, the person we choose will be a direct reflection of *us.*' Maria grimaced at the thought, then continued. 'In light of recent developments, we have removed both Annabella and Billie from the programme permanently. But of course, as is our way, we shall persevere. As a result of the last few days, we'll still be going ahead with the interview stages. Although now, there'll only be two of you in the running – yourself, and I believe you know the second person.'

So, Theo *had* got himself off the hook. Of course he had – all he needed to do was turn on that Theo Atwick golden-boy charm, and he'd have the whole programme wrapped around his little finger. Maria gestured to the door behind me, where Theo was entering the classroom.

Except it wasn't Theo.

It was Oliver.

I nearly choked. I was certain my eyes must've been deceiving me, but there was Oliver, strolling in like he owned the place. Maria politely handed me a glass of water while he took his seat beside me, a winning smile pasted onto his face. They both waited for my coughing fit to subside.

'I'm sorry,' I uttered, once I could finally catch a breath. 'I'm a little confused.'

'I'm sure you are,' Oliver said. Maria might have thought he sounded friendly, but I could hear the cloying smugness in his tone. I ignored him and tried again.

'What about Theo?' I asked Maria. Oliver visibly tensed at the sound of his (former?) best friend's name.

'I understand you must have some questions,' Maria said. 'Theo *was* in the race, but numerous allegations have been made concerning his conduct and, while I don't believe them to be in the same vein as the accusations made about the other candidates, it hardly reflects the standards we have for graduates of Rising Stars.'

Maria blinked her stress away, clearing her throat before offering us a tight smile.

'It's been a very quick turnaround, but we had to act fast to keep things moving in the right direction. With all the *unsavoury behaviour* that's been going on recently, the judges had to make the tough but necessary decision not to allow Theo,

Annabella *or* Billie to continue in the race in any capacity.'

And just like that, two more people were wiped out from the race. My mind whirled with possibilities, trying to build an image out of my confusion as to who could be behind this. With this new poster vigilante apparently on the loose and out for chaos, the chances of them striking again were high. But what could possibly be next?

'We thought things were over before they'd really had a chance to start,' Maria continued, 'but then Oliver came forward and reminded us of his fabulous application.'

Maria smiled in Oliver's direction, and he returned it, his smarm dialled up to its maximum.

'It's an honour to be given the opportunity,' he said. It made me feel sick, but Maria nodded her approval.

'So, the interview stage will still be going ahead, although we've moved it to early next week in order for you both – particularly you, Oliver – to prepare,' she said. 'I know it's such late notice, but I'm sure you'll be just fine.'

'I'll do my best,' Oliver replied. 'I know how important it is to find the right candidate, so it's a privilege to even be a part of this.'

I was flailing for something to say, to try and save this. If I let it carry on without interjecting, Oliver would worm his way into the programme. But I was drawing a blank, still stunned that it'd been him to walk into the classroom.

Maria, meanwhile, appeared delighted.

I said nothing.

'Well, if there are no questions, I wish you both the best of luck,' Maria finished. 'And I'll see you next week for your interviews!'

Oliver stood and shook her hand, then started for the door. In a daze, I mumbled a thank you and got up to leave too. Out in the corridor, Oliver was waiting for me. I tried to walk around him, but he stepped into my path, peering over my shoulder to make sure Maria hadn't followed.

'Got a nice little surprise there, huh?' he said in a low voice. 'Weren't expecting me to appear?'

'Something like that,' I murmured.

'Well, get used to it. Or don't. I'm not bothered

either way. But just know this.' He stepped forward so there was barely any space between us. 'I *will* win this because I deserve to. You won't take this from me again.'

Again. He was still holding a grudge that I'd taken *his* spot in the race, even though three of his friends could also be blamed for that. I guess they weren't here now – they'd been pushed aside. Which just left Oliver, stepping out of their shadows, ready to take it all.

Convenient?

Or planned?

Was it simply a coincidence that, out of four candidates, I was the only one who hadn't had a secret revealed about them yet? Or was it that the person responsible for it all, pulling strings like a puppet master, didn't know me well enough to know my secrets? But that wouldn't matter. If the culprit knew secrets about the other three and eliminated them from the race, that just left little old me to beat. That wouldn't be a problem, would it? Not for someone who already thought they were better than me in every way.

Not for the person standing in front of me right now.

It clicked in that moment – it *had* to be Oliver behind everything: the blog posts, the poster, the threat on my life. I had seen first hand how gutted he was about being left in the shadows while his friends basked in the spotlight. How utterly furious he was when someone he deemed unworthy – me – had taken the place he'd wanted so badly. And he *had* wanted it. I'd seen how tense he'd been, sitting in the crowd alone, waiting for his name to be called. And it never came. Had I really been stupid enough to assume he'd let this go without fighting back?

I tried to keep my face straight, but Oliver's eyes narrowed. I didn't want to alert him to my train of thought, so I made to step around him again. He moved into my path one more time, forcing me to look at him.

'Watch yourself, Harley.'

He didn't so much as blink. He stared me down for a few seconds, then turned to go, leaving me alone in the corridor. I thought about going back and telling Maria, but that felt like snitching, and

I had some morals, even if I was scared. Instead, I counted to ten, slowing my breathing down. Then I waited another thirty seconds to be sure Oliver had gone before heading for the stairs.

I wandered down the corridor towards the stairs, lost in my thoughts about what I was going to do now that I'd figured it all out. I'd need proof first, and that was going to be nearly impossible to find. But surely there had to be *something* that Oliver hadn't thought of, one tiny little detail he'd missed.

As I reached the top of the stairs, I suddenly sensed that I wasn't alone. It was a small sound that alerted me, a shuffle, like someone getting closer.

But I didn't have the chance to turn around.

I felt strong hands in the centre of my back, shoving me with full force, and before I knew it, I was tilting forward. I didn't even have time to scream out for help. It all happened so quickly and yet, somehow, in slow motion at the same time. It was like the seconds were stretching themselves, creeping ahead then jolting past in a blur.

The world began to turn upside down.

I could feel myself falling.

I tried to reach out for something, anything, but there was nothing except air and gravity greedily pulling me towards the ground. I couldn't stop it.

The last second stretched longer than the ones before it, taunting me with its finality. This was it. This was how it all ended. This second was all I had left.

And then everything went black.

I woke up to the rhythmic sound of my heartbeat. I was confused for a moment, blearily looking all around me at the white room that definitely didn't belong to me or my house. I tried to sit up, but my body protested, aching from head to toe. I groaned, clutching my ribs.

Ouch.

Where was I? Was I dreaming? If I rolled over and closed my eyes, would I wake up back in my own house? A haunting feeling told me I'd still be here, which just confused me more. I took in the bed and the pale blue curtain around it, the scratchy gown I was wearing, the machines hooked up to my body.

I was in hospital.

But how? Why? I tried to think back to the last thing I remembered, but all I could recall was my geography lesson, going to the front office to call my dad ... the posters about Billie. My breaths started to shallow, heartbeat climbing. That was it. Everything else was a blank. When I tried to pull any memory after that from my mind, all I could see was ... nothing.

'Ah, Mr Matthews,' a kind voice said.

I turned my aching neck to see an older man, greying at the temples and with glasses perched on the edge of his nose, stepping through the curtain. He wore green scrubs and carried a clipboard, which he was assessing with little flicks of his eyes.

'How are you feeling, Harley?'

'I ... I ... What happened?' I choked out.

The doctor frowned but tried to quickly smooth it away from his face. I started to panic.

'You're in the hospital, Harley. You had an accident earlier today. A woman by the name of Maria Turner found you at the bottom of a flight of stairs in your school and called an ambulance. But you're okay.' The doctor gave me a friendly smile and checked his notes. 'Your parents are downstairs in the canteen. I'm sure they'll be up in a minute. But for now, would you mind answering a few questions for me?'

In a blur, I told the doctor my name, my date of birth, the names of my parents, the month of the year, what school I went to. It seemed silly to begin with, until I realized the doctor was subtly checking my memory. When he asked if I could remember what had happened, I wracked my brain once more, but came up short.

'I'd expect some bruising over the next few days,' the doctor concluded. 'We're also running tests for possible concussion. There seems to be some short-term memory loss, but that might not be permanent. Things could come back to you over the next day or two. But the main thing is that you're okay. You got lucky.'

I wasn't sure if *lucky* was how I'd put it. It currently felt like the ambulance Maria called had run me over instead. Twice. I fell back into the bed, trying to steady myself with deep breaths. The doctor had promised I'd be okay with a few days of rest and recovery, and as my parents let themselves back into the room and showered me with hugs and kisses, I believed him.

So why did I still feel on edge?

It was a few hours later, while I was waiting for my test results to come back so I could be discharged, when Maria appeared in the doorway. She gave me a sympathetic smile, taking the chair next to my bed. I tried to sit up, groaning under my breath as I did.

'Hey, Harley. How are you feeling?'

'I've definitely been better,' I joked.

Maria laughed. 'Are your parents around?'

'They've gone home to fetch me some things in case I need to stay overnight.' Maria looked concerned for a second, but I quickly reassured her. 'It's unlikely – we're just waiting for the test results to come back and then I can go.'

Maria sighed with relief. 'You gave me such a fright. I left the classroom a few minutes after our talk and you were just there, at the bottom of the stairs, murmuring incoherently and barely conscious. I called the ambulance straight away. I'm just glad to see you're doing okay now.'

I blushed. Even though this had been a serious accident, I still felt embarrassed at the idea of Maria finding me, mumbling things I couldn't even remember.

'Thanks for, you know, calling the ambulance and everything,' I said quietly.

Maria waved off my gratitude. 'Don't be silly. I'm just glad I found you when I did. I had to come and make sure you were doing okay.'

We lapsed into a small silence for a moment, my brain running a hundred miles an hour, desperately trying to find any memory that might help me remember what had happened. But it felt like I was trying to stitch together a story when I didn't have all the pieces.

'What were we talking about in the classroom?' I mumbled, embarrassed that I even had to ask. 'Sorry, I just don't remember.'

Maria looked sympathetic. 'It was just a chat about the next steps for the Rising Stars programme. I told you about the interviews, which will take place next week. Although of *course* we'll happily postpone them while you're recovering! I'm sure Oliver won't mind.'

Oliver's name felt like ice-cold water dousing me from head to toe.

'O-Oliver was there?' I tried to keep my voice steady, but it hitched as I spoke.

Maria nodded. 'Yep! He's been accepted as a new candidate for the programme.'

I hesitated, worried to even think my next question in case it made it real. But I had to know. The pieces I was missing were starting to come back to me.

'You said I was talking incoherently when you found me?'

'You were,' Maria replied. 'It was difficult to make out at first, especially since I was more focused on calling for help. But when I knelt down beside you, you kept saying the same name over and over.'

I braced myself, my jaw clenched around my final question.

'Whose name was I saying?'

Maria paused; then she sent my world into freefall.

PETER

Harley Matthews was pushed down a flight of stairs. It had been the talk of Hardbridge Academy for days now, gossip and whispers flying through the corridors. Even now, after the weekend had flown by in a summery daze, people still couldn't let it go.

Billie was probably grateful. News of Harley's fall had overshadowed the posters about her being behind the blog posts in the first place, not to mention her penchant for stealing. I hadn't seen her since the day the posters came out. I guessed she was lying low, hoping people would just forget.

As for the other members of the Perfect Four, they still didn't seem to be talking to each other.

Annabella had settled into her new group of girls, who probably feared her more than they actually liked her, while Theo hung out with the boys from football now that he didn't have Oliver to fall back on. And speaking of the devil, Oliver had broken up with Violet, although that was to be expected. He obviously believed the rumours that his girlfriend and best friend were having a secret relationship behind his back.

Meanwhile, I was back to being alone in the halls of Hardbridge Academy, waiting for Harley to return to school and save me from boredom. I was excited to have him back, not least because, if the rumours were true, it looked like he might win the place on the Rising Stars programme after all. Oliver was still in the running, but someone claimed to have overheard the judges at lunch sympathizing with Harley's situation, saying he was a talented artist who deserved a shot. *An underdog*, they called him. Apparently one of the judges had also said that it wouldn't harm Rising Stars' reputation if a student who'd had a near-death experience got a life-changing dream in return. *A good story*, was how they were putting it, according to the gossip I'd heard. I wouldn't tell Harley that bit, but I *knew* all along that he could do it. Battling the Perfect Four single-handedly and coming out on top? What a hero.

First lesson on Monday morning was art, where Mr Briggs despaired at my attempt at drawing a vase of flowers. Sure, I was hardly going to give Van Gogh a run for his money, but Mr Briggs was pretty brutal in his feedback.

'Let's just say that art is a calling not everybody receives,' he said, the kindness in his tone not quite counterbalancing his words.

'I like to think of it as interpretive,' I tried, as the rest of the class packed up their things and began to leave. 'As in, you use your artistic eye to interpret the art in whatever way you see fit. You know, like clouds or whatever. Everybody will see something different.'

Mr Briggs smiled. 'Peter, I interpret that to be utter rubbish, but you get an A for coming up with that excuse.'

Wow, savage.

'I guess I won't be a Harley Matthews anytime soon,' I muttered, standing up and packing my bag.

'Ah, yes, Hardbridge Academy's finest artist.' Mr Briggs glowed in the direction of his display wall, which was mostly taken up by Harley's work. 'He'll go far one day, I'm sure.'

'Well, yeah, he'll win his place on the Rising Stars programme and the rest will be history. And he'll have you to thank! Honestly, sir, you should think about charging him ten per cent for getting him this far.'

Mr Briggs laughed, but it quickly fell short, his brow creasing.

'Me to thank?'

Now it was my turn to frown. I knew it was Monday morning and everybody was tired, but surely Mr Briggs knew what I was talking about.

'Uh, yeah? You know, putting Harley's name forward for the programme? If it wasn't for you, he wouldn't . . .'

I trailed off as I watched Mr Briggs's face cloud with confusion. 'Peter, what on earth are you talking about? I didn't put Harley's name forward for the programme. As a teacher, that would be crossing the line. If Harley was put forward as a candidate, it's because he did it himself.'

Mr Briggs checked his watch.

'Now, shouldn't you be getting on to your next class? You're about to be la—' The bell rang right on cue. Mr Briggs raised an eyebrow. 'Feel free to tell your next teacher that I kept you behind for five minutes to stop you getting into any trouble.'

'Thanks, sir,' I murmured, heading for the door.

As I walked through the emptying corridors in the direction of maths, I couldn't shake what Mr Briggs had said from my mind. He seemed pretty adamant that he hadn't put Harley's name forward, which would be a strange thing to lie about. But if that was the case, then why would Harley lie either?

I reached my locker, punching in the combination and throwing in my sketchpad. But as I grabbed the heavy maths textbook I needed for second lesson, a piece of paper caught my eye. It was the poster about Billie Bradley. 'GAME OVER', the title announced.

I read it through again, then once more, a hazy thought coming into focus the more I mulled over the words. I couldn't quite grasp it, but I had this *feeling* that something wasn't right. I only had the slip of paper because Harley had given it to me in the first place, and I . . .

Wait.

Harley had given me the poster. He'd taken it from his rucksack and handed it to me at lunch when I'd got back to school from the dentist. What had he said? That he'd been on his way back to class when he found the posters, the latest scandal waiting to be discovered.

But . . .

Would someone have had time to do that? He was on the phone to his dad for thirty seconds at most and in reception for an extra minute or two. He was gone from class for, what, five minutes at most? Surely that couldn't be enough time for someone to escape from their own class, throw the posters everywhere, tape them up on lockers and then disappear again before Harley returned.

Now my mind was jumping from one conclusion

to the next. The phone call itself, it had been so short. Almost unbelievably so. Harley said his dad always used the house phone, made out that he was some kind of technophobe who couldn't keep up with modern times and hated texting. Then he'd turned his back, said two sentences and hung up. Again, the timing just didn't make sense. Would his dad have been able to explain what was going on so quickly that the call would be over in half a minute? It seemed unlikely now I really thought about it.

So, did Harley even make the phone call? Or was it just an excuse to get out of class?

Everybody had been so focused on the downfall of the Perfect Four, me included, that nobody had paid attention to the person left standing in their wake, ready to win the only place on the Rising Stars programme. Except, Harley hadn't been the only one. He *thought* he would be, with Theo, Annabella and Billie out of the way. But the judges had pulled Oliver into the mix, putting everything into jeopardy. There was no longer any guarantee that Harley would win.

Except . . . the fall. Weren't the rumours already suggesting that the judges had been overheard saying they felt sorry for Harley and that he deserved a shot. Was the fall just that? A ploy to gain sympathy? Had it even happened at all?

Breathless, mind racing, I tried to gather my thoughts. Surely Harley wouldn't do this. He wouldn't. He hadn't even wanted to be a part of the programme in the first place. What did he say? *The programme has two places available. There's almost two hundred people in our year. You do the maths. I'd rather save myself the disappointment.* Proof he didn't want to be a part of this. Right?

Unless he wanted people to think that. Maybe he wanted people to assume he was the helpless victim, tied up in the games of the Perfect Four.

I told myself I had to be wrong. I even felt *guilty* for suspecting Harley could be capable of doing any of the things I'd just thought. But a little voice in the back of my head told me there might be more truth to my suspicions than I'd hoped. There was only one way to find out.

I'd seen Harley's locker combination the

morning after the blog post about Annabella went live, when we debriefed about the gossip and he told me about Mr Briggs putting his name forward. *A lie.* I'd been leaning next to him and my eyes couldn't help it – they watched his hands as they put in the code. I might not have remembered it, except I recalled thinking, *What an easy locker combination. He should probably change that.* 9876. Counting backwards. Hardly original, although better than 1111.

I checked all around me to make sure I was alone. Considering I was already ten minutes late for maths, the corridor was empty. Ignoring every rational thought in my head that told me to stop, I slammed my locker shut and moved down the row, stopping by number 404. I took a deep breath and then, with shaking fingers, entered the combination.

The locker swung open, revealing a bunch of textbooks, broken pencils, a few library books. On the surface, nothing unusual. I thought about shutting the door and going on about my day, forgetting everything. But my hands started sifting through the books, moving things around, searching for *anything* that would confirm or deny my suspicions.

Nothing.

Of course.

I was being stupid.

I was about to close the locker when I knocked something over. The packet fell out onto the floor, bursting open and sending fragments scattering everywhere. I swore under my breath and quickly dropped to a crouch, gathering it all up. I groaned to myself when I realized it was chalk and I was getting it all over my school trousers.

I stood up, about to throw the packet back into the locker, and froze.

Chalk.

What the outline of Harley's body had been drawn with at the bottom of those stairs after his name was announced as a candidate for the programme. He'd told me about it himself, how much it had freaked him out when he later found the outline and its sinister message gone. But when I'd suggested he tell a teacher, he'd said he didn't want to make it a bigger deal than it already was, which was silly because someone had apparently been threatening his safety.

'Oh my god . . .' I whispered.

What if *he* had drawn it himself? Told me about it to make sure I knew, so when he 'fell' down the stairs to gain some sympathy and secure his place on the programme, I would be able to back up his story that someone had threatened him in the first place.

And the obvious person to blame would be Oliver, the only competitor left who could take his dream away from him.

'What are you doing in my locker, Peter?'

I spun around, dropping the packet of chalk again. Harley was standing behind me, so close, there was barely any space between us. I tried to back up, but the lockers penned me in. His face was smoothed of any emotion, but there was a faint twitch at the corner of his mouth. I stuttered, searching for something, *anything*, to say. But I couldn't find any words.

'Looks a little like breaking the law to me,' Harley

answered in my silence. He glanced at a locker a few places down, eyes narrowing, then turned his attention back on me, putting a firm hand on my shoulder like we were still friends. 'Gaining access to my locker, going through my things.' Harley smiled. 'You're acting a little suspicious, Peter.'

I shook my head, trying to rearrange my thoughts. 'I know what you've done, Harley,' I said, fighting to keep my voice even. 'It's *you*.'

Harley's hand dropped from my shoulder, lingering for just a second before he took a few steps back. He glanced down the hallway, no doubt checking to make sure we were alone.

'I'm not entirely sure what you're talking about, Peter. I mean, it was *you* who so desperately wanted to be in the running for the Rising Stars programme. Everybody knew you wanted it, and how gutted you must've been when you were left out. And that's why you befriended me, isn't it? To get close, so you could figure out how to worm your way in.'

I shook my head, my mouth falling open, words struggling to come out.

'That . . . that's not what happened. I know what you did, Harley.' He looked at me expectantly, one eyebrow quirked. I shook my head, as if that would get my jumbled thoughts in order, then started to tell what I was almost certain was the truth.

'I know Mr Briggs didn't put you forward for the programme. You did it yourself, but you wanted people to believe that you'd already given up. Who would suspect you of anything when you didn't want to be a part of the competition in the first place?' I paused, but Harley didn't say a word, so I continued. 'You wanted to take the Perfect Four down, and you needed something that would get them thrown off the shortlist. Or maybe just something that would put a mark against their name so the judges would pick you over them. It didn't have to be true, just gossip that you knew people would believe. You must have been behind the blog posts. That's why your secrets were never revealed. But you knew you couldn't get away completely untouched – that would be too unbelievable.'

94

I frowned, a memory materializing in my mind and a new suspicion revealing itself.

'You made the posters blaming Billie and had them ready to go. But you needed to get out of class to plant them, so you ducked into the cupboard in geography and … I guess, you called reception, pretending to be your dad with an emergency. In the silence of the classroom, I thought I'd heard you speaking in the cupboard, which I thought was strange, but I just assumed you were talking to yourself.'

The corner of Harley's mouth flickered with a smirk. My breaths shortened, trapped in a swell of panic, but I couldn't stop now.

'You'd made it look like the Perfect Four were at each other's throats, tearing themselves apart. With the coast clear, you just needed to look like you'd also been targeted. Let me guess –' I nodded down at the packet of chalk on the floor, my heart hammering as I pieced it all together – 'you drew your own outline and made sure to tell me so you'd have back-up that someone had been threatening you. And then the fall itself. No serious injuries?

Seems lucky. Or maybe you just staged the whole thing so it *looked* like you fell. Oliver coming into the picture was perfect because now you had someone with a motive to actually hurt you and get you out of the way. It would seal their fate ... and yours.'

A chill ran down my spine as I finished. My mouth was dry, and my hands were shaking with anxious adrenaline. I knew I was right. I didn't have proof, but I had to be. It all made sense.

'It was all you,' I finished.

Harley watched me closely, unblinking for a long, drawn-out moment. Then, inexplicably, he broke out into a grin and started to clap, each slow collision of his hands setting my heart on edge.

'You really had it all figured out. No, really, I'm impressed. But ... I don't like that story.'

My heart dropped. 'W-what?'

'That's not the truth, is it, Peter?' It was a taunt, one that put my whole world on a knife's edge. I could sense danger, but I didn't know where it was coming from. 'Maybe it was *you* who had all the intel on the Perfect Four. You didn't even have to tell the truth necessarily – you just had to plant that seed of doubt with your little blog posts, and other people couldn't *wait* to latch on to any piece of gossip that'd bring our school royalty down. But maybe you didn't have anything on me. I was the one you couldn't figure out how to get rid of. Soooo ...' Harley tapped his chin, thinking to himself. 'Let's say you tried to freak me out with the chalk outline to warn me away. But when that didn't work ... you did it for real. You pushed me.'

'Y-you're ly—' I tried to stutter, but Harley continued.

'It's such a shame I don't really remember what happened that day. I must've hit my head pretty hard. Except ... the judge who found me, she remembered me saying a name when I was barely conscious. I kept repeating it over and over. And that name was Oliver. But, in my defence, I was confused – I'd just been pushed down the stairs after all! You were with me before the meeting, so maybe you hid in the shadows and waited for your chance to get rid of me. And maybe the name I should've been saying when I was found was … yours.'

I was in freefall, incapable of saving myself. My mouth hung open but no words came out, any defence or fight-back trapped in my throat.

'And now, here you are, breaking into my locker and planting evidence. Hoping to get away with it?' Harley looked down the corridor and when he turned back, he offered me a sad smile, as if he was truly sorry for what was about to happen next. 'This was meant for someone else, but I guess you can have it now. Call it a little gift for solving everything.' He began to well up, tears brimming in his eyes. 'Check your pockets,' he whispered. 'You've got mail.'

The floor felt like it was tilting beneath me. I dug my hands into my trouser pockets and found nothing. I tried my blazer pockets, and that's when my fingers brushed against something small.

'The original blogs and poster had to come from somewhere,' Harley said as I grasped it and pulled out a tiny device. 'And it looks like that *somewhere* is right there, in your hand.'

Before I could react, several people rushed through the doors at the end of the corridor and Harley started to cry in earnest, loud sobs as he pointed a finger in my direction.

'It was him!' he howled, scrambling backwards as if *I* was the threat. 'I remember! He was the one who pushed me down the stairs. And now he's breaking into my locker with ... with some kind of memory stick!'

I looked at the device in my palm, panic rising and threatening to drown me. Sure enough, in my hand I held a memory stick. One that I was positive Harley had planted in my pocket when he moved his hand from my shoulder.

'I didn't ...' I tried as two police officers arrived and separated us.

'We have some questions we'd like to ask you, Peter McGregor,' one of them said, his voice steely. 'But as you're a minor, we'll need to call your parents first.'

In my panic, I couldn't find the words to defend myself. I weakened in the police officer's grasp, letting him lead me away. But before we walked through the door, I glanced back down the hallway to where Harley was being consoled by another officer as well as Mrs Hansen, our headteacher. He looked me in the eye, tears staining his cheeks. And with everybody's back turned, he smiled.

Harley Matthews had finally won.

LOOK OUT FOR
BENJAMIN DEAN'S
NEXT KILLER THRILLER

Bury Your Friends

COMING
AUGUST 2025

HAPPY WORLD BOOK DAY!

BOOST YOUR WELLBEING

Choosing to read in your free time can help make you happier and more successful.

Now you've read this book:

- **SWAP** it

- **TALK** about it

- **RECOMMEND** it to a friend

- **READ** it again

- **EXPLORE** similar books you'd like to read

DISCOVER more at **WORLDBOOKDAY.COM**

You can also visit your local library or nearest bookshop for ideas on what to read next.

Changing lives through a love of books and reading.

READ YOUR WAY

WORLD BOOK DAY®

Celebrate World Book Day by reading what YOU want in YOUR free time!

BENJAMIN DEAN is a full-time author with a background in celebrity journalism. He has interviewed a host of glitzy celebrities and broke the news that Rihanna can't wink (she blinks, in case you were wondering). His award-winning middle-grade debut, *Me, My Dad and the End of the Rainbow*, was described as 'One of the most joyful books you'll read this year' (The Bookseller), and he's since gone on to publish *The Secret Sunshine Project*, as well *The King is Dead*, *How to Die Famous* and *This Story is a Lie* (for the Independent Readers category in World Book Day 2025) for older readers. Benjamin can be found on Twitter as @notagainben tweeting about Rihanna and LGBTQ+ culture to his 10,000+ followers.